Dear Parents:

Congratulations! Your child is taking the first steps on an exciting journey. The destination? Independent reading!

STEP INTO READING® will help your child get u̱ ˌne program offers five steps to reading success. Each step includes fun stories and colorful art or photographs. In addition to original fiction and books with favorite characters, there are Step into Reading Non-Fiction Readers, Phonics Readers and Boxed Sets, Sticker Readers, and Comic Readers—a complete literacy program with something to interest every child.

Learning to Read, Step by Step!

Ready to Read   Preschool–Kindergarten
• big type and easy words • rhyme and rhythm • picture clues
For children who know the alphabet and are eager to begin reading.

Reading with Help   Preschool–Grade 1
• basic vocabulary • short sentences • simple stories
For children who recognize familiar words and sound out new words with help.

Reading on Your Own   Grades 1–3
• engaging characters • easy-to-follow plots • popular topics
For children who are ready to read on their own.

Reading Paragraphs   Grades 2–3
• challenging vocabulary • short paragraphs • exciting stories
For newly independent readers who read simple sentences with confidence.

Ready for Chapters   Grades 2–4
• chapters • longer paragraphs • full-color art
For children who want to take the plunge into chapter books but still like colorful pictures.

STEP INTO READING® is designed to give every child a successful reading experience. The grade levels are only guides; children will progress through the steps at their own speed, developing confidence in their reading. The F&P Text Level on the back cover serves as another tool to help you choose the right book for your child.

Remember, a lifetime love of reading starts with a single step!

Visit us on the Web!
StepIntoReading.com
randomhousekids.com

Educators and librarians, for a variety of teaching tools, visit us at
RHTeachersLibrarians.com

Library of Congress Cataloging-in-Publication Data
Depken, Kristen L.
Tawny, scrawny lion / by Kristen L. Depken ; illustrated by Sue DiCicco.
pages cm. — (Step into reading. Level 1.)
"Adapted from the beloved Little Golden Book written by Kathryn Jackson and illustrated by Gustaf Tenggren."
Summary: "A family of ten rabbits teaches a hungry lion to eat carrot stew—so that he won't eat them!" — Provided by publisher.
ISBN 978-1-101-93424-1 (pb) — ISBN 978-1-101-93425-8 (glb) — ISBN 978-0-553-53993-6 (ebook)
[1. Lion—Fiction. 2. Rabbits—Fiction. 3. Animals—Fiction.]
I. DiCicco, Sue, illustrator. II. Jackson, Kathryn. Tawny, scrawny lion. III. Title.
PZ7.D4396Taw 2016
[E]—dc23
2015012696

Printed in the United States of America
10 9 8 7 6 5 4 3 2 1

This book has been officially leveled by using the F&P Text Level Gradient™ Leveling System.

TAWNY SCRAWNY LION

Adapted from the beloved Little Golden Book
written by Kathryn Jackson and illustrated by Gustaf Tenggren

by Kristen L. Depken
illustrated by Sue DiCicco

Random House 🏠 New York

The tawny, scrawny lion
is always hungry.

Run, run, run!
He chases monkeys
on Monday.

Kangaroos on Tuesday.

He chases zebras
on Wednesday.

Bears on Thursday.

Camels on Friday.

Elephants on Saturday.

Run, run, run!
The lion is still hungry!

"Stop chasing us!"
say the animals.

"Stop running,"
says the lion.

Hop, hop, hop.
A brave little rabbit
talks to the lion.
"You look scrawny,"
he says.

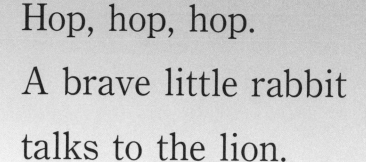

So he asks the lion
to eat supper
with his family.
Carrot stew!

Carrot stew?

Yuck!

Rabbits?

Yum!

The lion says yes.

The lion follows
the rabbit.

Herbs and berries!
The rabbit picks some
for dinner.

Then he stops
to catch fish
for the stew.

19

At last
they reach
the rabbit's house.

The lion is so hungry!

The lion sees something
he would like to eat!
More rabbits!

Hop, hop, hop!
The rabbits bring the lion
some carrot stew.

It smells good.

It tastes good.

The lion eats bowl

after bowl!

Time for berries!
The lion eats
lots of berries,
too.

The tawny, scrawny lion
is not scrawny anymore!

The lion walks home.
He is good and fat
and full.

He will not eat
animals anymore.

The animals are
so happy!
They thank
the little rabbit.

But what will
the tawny lion
eat now?

More carrot stew!